For Noona

First published 2014 by Walker Books Ltd
87 Vauxhall Walk, London SE11 5HJ

2 4 6 8 10 9 7 5 3 1

This book has been typeset in Mrs Ant

Printed in China

British Library Cataloguing in Publication Data:
a catalogue record for this book is available from the British Library

ISBN 978-1-4063-5845-2

www.walker.co.uk

If I Could Choose

Matt Phelan

WALKER BOOKS
AND SUBSIDIARIES
LONDON • BOSTON • SYDNEY • AUCKLAND

It was raining.

And raining.

And RAINING.

“I’m bored,”
said Penelope.

"If you could choose, what would
you do?" asked her daddy.

"Do you mean *anything*?"

"Yes, I mean anything at all –
if you could choose."

“Well, if I could choose…

I would go to the zoo."

Ooo-ooo-ooo!

“If I could choose…

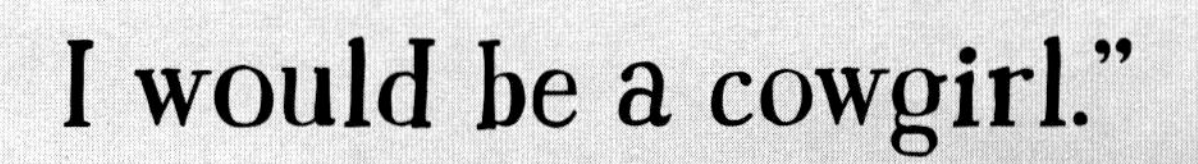
I would be a cowgirl."

Howdy-do!

“If I could choose…

I would be a pirate captain.

AND...

we would sail to the island of dinosaurs!

The pirate ship would also be a rocket.

And we would fly to the moon…

FOR THE BIGGEST

MOON PARTY EVER!

But I guess if I could *really* choose…

it would rain tomorrow, too."